The Misadventures of Miles and Maya

Juneteenth Odyssey

By Renee Marie

Dedication

This book, Miles and Maya: Juneteenth Odyssey,' is lovingly and respectfully dedicated to my ancestors.

To those who lived through the struggle, who endured the harsh chains of enslavement, whose spirits were unbroken in the face of adversity. To those who celebrated the first taste of freedom on that significant day in June and those who carried the torch forward, keeping the stories and traditions alive.

Your resilience, bravery, and unwavering hope echo through the ages, reminding us of our roots and the journey our people have made. Your legacy inspires us and shapes our understanding of freedom, equality, and justice.

This is a tribute to your strength, courage, and enduring love, which have guided us through the generations. As we honor Juneteenth, we honor you. Your stories are still remembered. Your histories are our guiding light. Your lives matter yesterday, today, and always."

INTRODUCTION

Welcome to Book 2 of the thrilling The Misadventure of Miles and Maya series, ' Miles and Maya: Juneteenth Odyssey.' Our intrepid explorers, Miles, and Maya are back! This time, they are set to uncover the rich history and enduring significance of a special day in American history – Juneteenth.

Their journey will take them back in time, through struggle and triumph, as they learn about the proclamation of Emancipation and its belated arrival in Texas. They'll witness the first Juneteenth celebrations and understand why this day, often called Freedom Day or Emancipation Day, holds such immense importance for African Americans.

As Miles and Maya navigate the pages of history, they will also experience the vibrant traditions of present- day Juneteenth celebrations – the music, the feasts, the parades, and the stories that make this day a symbol of resilience and freedom.

Join Miles and Maya as they embark on this illuminating journey.
Along the way, you'll laugh, wonder and learn.
So, buckle up and get ready to dive into the
inspiring saga of Juneteenth!

Chapter 1

The Mysterious Invitation

It was a warm summer afternoon when Miles and Maya tore through the house, returning from their last day of school. Their summer vacation had finally begun, and the siblings were eager for adventure. As they kneel with their book bags on the living room floor, a mysterious envelope fell out of Maya's bag.

"Hey, what's this?" Miles asked, retrieving the envelope. It was made of thick, cream-colored paper, sealed with a wax stamp.

Maya shrugged. "I don't know. Open it."

You're Invited to our
Juneteenth Celebration
June 19, 2024
3:00 PM
Freedom Park

Miles carefully broke the seal and pulled out a beautifully designed invitation. It read, "You are cordially invited to the Annual Juneteenth Celebration at Freedom Park.
Come join us for a day of joy, freedom, and remembrance."

"Juneteenth?" Miles questioned; his eyebrows wrinkled in confusion. He turned to Maya, who also seemed puzzled.

"I think I've heard of it before," Maya said, her face. scrunched up. "Our history teacher mentioned it once, but I can't remember what it's about."

Miles nodded; his interest piqued.
"We should find out more about it."

Maya agreed, her eyes sparkling with curiosity.
"And we should go to this celebration.
It sounds like it could be fun."

With the mysterious invitation in hand and a newfound sense of excitement, the siblings began their quest to unravel the history and significance of Juneteenth. Little did they know, their journey would lead them to an unforgettable misadventure that would deepen their understanding of freedom and history.

Chapter 2
The History of Juneteenth

Miles and Maya woke up early the next day, their excitement about the upcoming celebration stirring them from sleep. After a quick breakfast, they sat down with their laptop, ready to discover the history of Juneteenth.

"What do we know so far?"
Miles asked as he opened the browser.

Maya replied, "We know it's a celebration, and it's related to history."

Miles typed 'Juneteenth' into the search bar, filling the screen with a wave of information. The siblings read aloud together, learning that Juneteenth, also known as Freedom Day or Emancipation Day, commemorated the end of slavery in the United States.

On June 19, 1865, Union General Gordon Granger arrived in Galveston, Texas, with the news that the Civil War had ended and the enslaved were now free. This was two years after President Abraham Lincoln's Emancipation Proclamation, which officially outlawed slavery. Texas, being remote and having a small union presence, was one of the last states to enforce the proclamation.

"It's like a second Independence Day,"
Maya said, her eyes wide with realization.

"Yeah," Miles agreed, "but it's specifically for
African Americans whose ancestors were enslaved.
It's a celebration of their freedom."

The siblings spent the rest of the morning reading stories of the day's celebration with music, food, and speeches. They learned about traditional foods like red velvet cake, the red representing the endurance and bloodshed of African Americans, and watermelon being eaten to celebrate freedom for the enslaved and hope for future prosperity.

Miles and Maya felt even more excited about attending the Juneteenth celebration with this knowledge. They could hardly wait to be part of this important day of remembrance and joy. Unbeknownst to them, the real adventure was just around the corner.

Chapter 3

The Significance of Juneteenth in American History

After their initial discovery, Miles and Maya decided to investigate the significance of Juneteenth in American history further. They visited their local library, where they befriended Ms. Ada, an elderly librarian with a passion for history.

As they sat down with Ms. Ada at a cozy corner of the library, she explained, "Juneteenth is not just a date in history, but a journey towards freedom and equality. It's a reminder of a past we must acknowledge and learn from."

She spoke of the struggle of African Americans post-Emancipation – how freedom didn't immediately translate to equality. They faced new forms of oppression like segregation, voter suppression, and racial violence. But she also spoke of resilience, unity, and progress.

"Juneteenth is celebrated as a triumph over these adversities," Ms. Ada said, her eyes gleaming with conviction. "It honors the strength and spirit of the African- American community."

She explained how the day has evolved, with generations adding their traditions and interpretations. Juneteenth became a time for family reunions, a chance to trace back roots, and a platform to educate others about African– American culture and history.

"But most importantly," Ms. Ada concluded, "it's a celebration of progress, a testament to how far we've come, and a reminder of how far we still have to go."

Miles and Maya left the library that day with a sense of reverence for Juneteenth. They understood that the celebration at Freedom Park was more than just a summer event – it symbolized a painful past, a resilient present, and a hopeful future. They looked forward to joining this celebration, now understanding its profound significance in American history. Unbeknownst to them, this was just the beginning of their journey.

Chapter 4

The Misadventure Begins

As the day of the Juneteenth celebration drew closer,
Miles and Maya decided to contribute to the event.
They brainstormed ideas and finally settled on creating a
banner that illustrated the journey from slavery to freedom
and everything they had learned about Juneteenth.

They spent days sketching and painting, their hands covered in
hues of green, reds, and yellows. They painted scenes of struggle,
resilience, and joy, their brush strokes pulsating with the energy
of the stories they had learned.

Finally, the day before Juneteenth, they finished their masterpiece.
They had never been prouder. But their excitement was
short-lived when they realized they had a problem:
the banner was too giant to fit in their dad's pickup truck,
their only available transport.

They panicked and called their friends, neighbors, and anyone
who could help, but everyone was busy preparing for the
celebration. As the sun began to set, they felt their spirits dampen.
Their beautiful banner, resulting from their hard work and
passion, might miss the celebration.

Just when they were about to give up, Miles had an idea.
"What about Mr. Johnson's tractor?" he suggested.
Mr. Johnson, their elderly neighbor, had an old tractor
that he used for his farm work.

With renewed hope, they rushed to Mr. Johnson's farmhouse.
After hearing their predicament, he agreed to help them
transport the banner early the following day.

Their problem was solved; Miles and Maya went to bed
that night tired but content, their dreams filled with anticipation
for the celebration. Little did they know, this was just the
beginning of their misadventures.

Chapter 5
The Helpful Stranger

On Juneteenth, they arrived with a warm breeze and a clear sky. Miles and Maya woke up early, eager to transport their banner to Freedom Park. They met Mr. Johnson at his farmhouse, where his tractor was ready for them.

As they loaded the banner onto the trailer attached to the tractor, they felt a sense of relief. Their artwork, a symbol of freedom and resilience, was finally on its way to the celebration.

They set off towards the park, the tractor rumbling along the dusty road. Along the way, they passed by fields of blooming flowers and chirping birds, filled with the scent of summer. Miles and Maya couldn't help but feel grateful for the beauty surrounding them.

However, their peaceful journey was soon interrupted by a loud bang. The tractor sputtered and came to a halt, smoke billowing from the engine. Mr. Johnson cursed under his breath, trying to assess the damage.

Miles and Maya exchanged worried glances. How were they going to transport the banner now? A voice called out just as they were about to resign themselves to another setback.

"Need a hand?"

They turned to see a young man walking towards them. He introduced himself as James, a mechanic passing by on his way to the celebration. Seeing their predicament, he offered to help fix the tractor.

With James' expertise, the tractor was up and running quickly. Miles, Maya, and Mr. Johnson thanked him profusely, overwhelmed by his kindness and generosity.

As they resumed their journey to Freedom Park, Miles smiled at Maya. "It seems like Juneteenth is not just a celebration of freedom but also a reminder of the kindness and unity that can help us overcome any obstacle."

Maya nodded in agreement, grateful for the helpful stranger they had encountered on their misadventure-filled journey. Little did they know, more surprises awaited them at the celebration.

Chapter 6

The Juneteenth Celebration

As Miles, Maya, and Mr. Johnson finally arrived at Freedom Park, a bustling crowd of people of all ages and backgrounds greeted them. The park was adorned with colorful decorations, and laughter and music filled the air. The spirit of celebration was palpable.

They carefully unloaded their banner from the trailer, setting it up in a prominent spot for everyone to see. As they stepped back to admire their work, they couldn't help but feel a sense of pride and accomplishment. The banner stood as a testament to the stories of struggle and triumph that Juneteenth represented.

They joined in the festivities throughout the day,
participating in dance performances, musical acts,
and storytelling sessions. They sampled delicious food from
various vendors, including traditional dishes honoring
African American heritage.

As the sun set, the celebration's highlight began: a reenactment
of the reading of the Emancipation Proclamation.
People gathered around a stage, their faces illuminated by the
flickering torches. A solemn hush fell over the crowd as a
local actor recited the words that had brought freedom to
millions of enslaved people.

Tears welled up in Maya's eyes as she listened to the powerful words that echoed through the park. She felt a deep connection to her ancestors' history and struggles and a sense of gratitude for the sacrifices they had made for future generations.

Miles squeezed Maya's hand in solidarity, and together, they watched as the crowd erupted into cheers and applause at the end of the reenactment. The sound of drums and trumpets filled the air, beginning a jubilant celebration of freedom and unity.

As the night wore on, Miles, Maya, and Mr. Johnson sat around the park bench, sharing stories and laughter with new friends they had made at the celebration. They felt a sense of belonging and community that warmed their hearts.

As the stars twinkled above them, Miles smiled at Maya. "This has been an unforgettable Juneteenth, filled with misadventures and surprises, but ultimately a celebration of freedom and unity."

Maya nodded, her heart full of gratitude for the experiences they had shared and the lessons they had learned. The misadventure that had begun as a simple desire to contribute to the celebration turned into a journey of discovery and connection, bringing them closer to their community and heritage.

And as they sat under the night sky,
surrounded by the sounds of joy.

Chapter 7

The Celebration Continues

The next morning, Miles, Maya, and Mr. Johnson woke up contented. The memories of the Juneteenth celebration lingered in their minds, filling them with a renewed sense of purpose and unity.

As they gathered around the breakfast table at Mr. Johnson's farmhouse, they reflected on the previous day's events. They shared stories of the people they had met, the dances they had learned, and the delicious food they had tasted.

Mr. Johnson smiled as he poured them cups of orange juice. "This has been one of the most memorable Juneteenth celebrations I've ever experienced. And it's all thanks to you two and your beautiful banner.

Miles, Maya and their Dad exchanged grateful glances, feeling proud of their contribution to the community. The banner, now a symbol of hope and resilience, had brought people together and sparked conversations about the importance of freedom and unity.

After breakfast, they decided to stroll through Freedom Park one last time before returning home. The park was quiet in the early morning light, a peaceful contrast to the lively festivities of the previous day.

As they walked, they came across their banner, still standing tall and vibrant against the park's backdrop. A few people stopped to admire it, taking in its intricate details and powerful message.

A young girl approached them, her eyes wide with wonder. "Did you make this?" she asked, pointing to the banner.

Miles and Maya nodded, smiling at her enthusiasm. "We did," Maya replied. "It's a symbol of freedom and resilience, inspired by the stories of Juneteenth."

The girl's face lit up with understanding, and she looked at the banner with newfound appreciation. "It's beautiful," she whispered.

Miles felt a sense of fulfillment wash over him as they continued their walk through the park. The misadventures, the challenges, and the moments of connection had all led them to this point, where their artwork had touched the hearts of others and inspired a new generation to learn about their history.

As they made their way back to Mr. Johnson's farmhouse, the sound of laughter and music from the park behind them, Miles knew that the spirit of Juneteenth would continue to live on in their hearts, guiding them towards a future filled with hope, unity, and celebration.

Chapter 8

Lessons Learned

As Miles, Maya, and Mr. Johnson returned to the farmhouse, they couldn't help but reflect on the lessons they had learned throughout their Juneteenth adventure.

Sitting on the porch, they shared stories and insights, each deepening their understanding of Juneteenth's significance and the importance of unity and resilience in the face of adversity.

Mr. Johnson spoke first, his voice filled with wisdom. "Juneteenth is not just a celebration of freedom, but a reminder of the struggles and sacrifices that came before. It's a time to honor our ancestors and the resilience of our community."

Miles nodded in agreement, his thoughts drifting to the people they had met and the stories they had heard. "We learned so much from the people we met along the way," he said. "Their stories of strength and perseverance inspired us to create something meaningful and lasting."

Maya added, "And our banner was a way to honor and share those stories with others. It's a testament to the power of art and community in preserving our history and celebrating our culture."

As the sun began to set, casting a warm glow over the farmhouse, they sat in companionable silence, each lost in their thoughts.

Finally, Miles spoke up, breaking the quiet. "The biggest lesson we've learned is that change begins with us. By coming together, sharing our stories, and creating something beautiful, we can inspire others to do the same."

Maya smiled, a sense of gratitude filling her heart. "And that's the beauty of Juneteenth. It's a celebration of the past and a call to action for the future. A future where freedom, unity, and resilience are at the forefront of everything we do."

As they sat together on the porch, laughter and music from the park drifted towards them, a reminder of the joy and togetherness that Juneteenth had brought to their community.

As they watched the sun dip below the horizon, casting a golden light over the fields, Miles, Maya, and Mr. Johnson knew that the lessons they had learned during their Juneteenth celebration would stay with them forever, guiding them toward a future filled with hope, unity, and endless possibilities.

Chapter 9

An Annual Tradition

As the days passed and summer turned to fall, Miles, Maya, and Mr. Johnson found themselves reminiscing about the Juneteenth celebration that had brought them together uniquely.

They had stayed in touch, sharing stories and updates on their lives, but they felt a longing for the sense of community and togetherness they had experienced at that time.

JUNETEENTH

One day, Miles had an idea as they sat around the kitchen table at Mr. Johnson's farmhouse. "What if we make the Juneteenth celebration an annual tradition?" he suggested, excitement bubbling in his voice.

Maya's eyes lit up with enthusiasm. "That's a wonderful idea! We could gather the community annually to celebrate freedom, unity, and resilience."

Mr. Johnson nodded in agreement. "It would be a beautiful way to honor our history and keep the spirit of Juneteenth alive for generations to come."

And so, they set to work planning the first annual Juneteenth celebration. They reached out to the community, inviting people to come together for a day of festivities, music, dance, and remembrance.

As the day of the celebration arrived, the park was filled with laughter and joy. People of all ages came together, sharing stories, food, and music as they honored Juneteenth's legacy and celebrated their community's strength and resilience.

Miles, Maya, and Mr. Johnson stood together, watching children play, elders share wisdom, and friends dance in the warm summer sun.

"This is what Juneteenth is all about," Mr. Johnson said, smiling.
"It's a day to come together, to remember our
past, and to celebrate our future."

Miles and Maya nodded in agreement, feeling proud and
grateful for the tradition they had helped to create.

As the sun set on the first annual Juneteenth celebration,
Miles, Maya, and Mr. Johnson knew this was just the beginning.
The spirit of unity, resilience, and hope that had brought them
together would continue to guide them in the years to come as
they honored their history and celebrated their community
with love and joy.

www.ingramcontent.com/pod-product-compliance
Lightning Source LLC
Chambersburg PA
CBHW042051110726
48006CB00002B/355